S0-AQC-510

Based on the teleplay "A Little Vacation"
by Mark Waxman

HarperCollins®, ♣®, HarperFestival®, and Festival Readers™
are trademarks of HarperCollins Publishers Inc.
Stuart Little: Spooky Surprise
Text and illustrations copyright © 2003 by Adelaide Productions, Inc.
Printed in the U.S.A. All rights reserved.
Library of Congress catalog card number: 2002112421.
www.harperchildrens.com
1 2 3 4 5 6 7 8 9 10

First Edition

STUART LITTLE™

Spooky Surprise

Adaptation by Amy Edgar

Illustrations by Jose Lopez

📙 HarperFestival®
A Division of HarperCollinsPublishers

Stuart Little was excited.

The Littles were going to spend a

weekend in the country with Uncle

Crenshaw.

They hoped it would stop raining.

In the backseat, Stuart and his
brother, George, made plans to
go swimming and hiking.
Martha, the littlest Little,
practiced making animal sounds.
"Baa, baa, baa," she said.

All the Littles were looking forward

to seeing Uncle Crenshaw.

Except Snowbell, the cat.

He already wished he'd stayed home.

Just when they thought they were
lost, the Littles spotted an inn.
"Is that where we're meeting
Uncle Crenshaw?" asked Mrs. Little.
"It looks haunted!" said Stuart. "Cool."

"Now, boys, you know there's no such thing as ghosts, right?" asked Mr. Little.

"Right," said George, but he was not so sure.

They knocked on the inn's door.

It swung wide open.

The Littles entered.

Then it slammed shut behind them.

Out of nowhere, a creepy old man appeared.

"Hello," said the man.

"I don't recall any reservations for this evening."

That's odd, thought Mr. Little. *Uncle Crenshaw said he had reserved our rooms.*

But since the Littles were his only guests, the innkeeper showed them to some rooms anyway.

"I guess Uncle Crenshaw is running late," said Mrs. Little.

"This place is spooky," said Stuart.

"We've got to go exploring!"

"Or we could stay here,"

replied George.

He didn't want to explore a

haunted inn.

The Littles were almost finished unpacking
when they noticed Snowbell was missing.
"We'll go look for him," volunteered Stuart.
"We will?" asked George.

"Sure, let's go," said Stuart, pulling George into the hallway.

"Snooowbell!" called the boys.

"Wait. I think I heard something,"
said George.

"It might be a ghost."

"There's no such thing as ghosts,"
said Stuart.

Seconds later, a furry white ball

came flying toward them.

"See, George," said Stuart.

"Nothing but a big white cat."

Just then, they heard footsteps.

Thump, thump, thump.

Who was coming?

Stuart, George, and Snowbell hid
themselves under a couch.
A pair of loafers came into view
and stopped right in front of them.

"Boys?" asked Mr. Little, as he shone a flashlight underneath the couch.

"Dad!" said Stuart and George.

They were more than a little relieved.

Back in their room, George and Stuart

climbed into bed.

It was nighttime, but they weren't

sleepy yet.

And where was Uncle Crenshaw?

"We haven't explored outside yet,"
said Stuart.

"Outside, in the rain?" asked George.

"Don't be such a scaredy cat,"
said Stuart.

The boys tiptoed past their
parents' room.

They headed out into the rainy night.

"I hope we find Uncle Crenshaw soon,"
said George.

Suddenly, a large hand grabbed

George's shoulder.

"Ahh!" yelled the boys.

"It's a ghost, and he's after us!"

They ran as fast as they could
toward the inn.

Lightning flashed.

The boys turned to see a hooded
figure chasing after them.

They flung the door open.

There stood Mr. and Mrs. Little
with Martha.

Before anyone could speak, the
figure ran up and pulled back his
hood.

"Uncle Crenshaw!" they shouted.

"I gave you bad directions," he said.

"The inn we were supposed to stay at
is down the lane."

A few minutes later,

the Littles were drinking hot

chocolate in front of the fireplace.

Stuart and George told Uncle

Crenshaw their "ghost" stories.

Soon, everyone was laughing.

"Oooooooooo."

"What was that?" asked George.

Then they all heard it again:

"Oooooooooo."

The Littles turned to see . . .

29

Martha giggling.

"Martha," said Stuart,

"a cow says, '*Mooooo*,' not '*Oooooo*.' "

Then they all laughed.

"George and I have pretty good imaginations," said Stuart. "The next time we take a trip, we'll have to let our imaginations take a vacation!"